To..............................

From..........................

Library of Congress catalog number: 2003106619
First published in Great Britain by Doubleday, a division of Transworld Publishers, 2000
First miniature edition published in Great Britain by Doubleday, 2002
Printed in Singapore
Designed by Ian Butterworth
First American edition, 2001
First American miniature edition, 2004
1 3 5 7 9 10 8 6 4 2

www.fsgkidsbooks.com

My Dad

Anthony Browne

FARRAR STRAUS GIROUX

New York

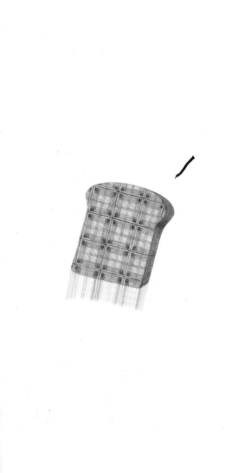

He's all right, my dad.

My dad isn't afraid of ANYTHING

even the Big Bad Wolf.

He can jump right over the moon

and walk on a tightrope
(without falling off).

He can wrestle with giants,

r win the   fathers' race on
sports day, easily.
He's all right, my dad.

My dad can eat like a horse,

and he can swim like a fish.

He's as strong as a gorilla,

...nd as happy as a hippopotamus.

He's all right,
my dad.

My dad's as big as a house,

and as soft as my teddy.

He's as wise as an owl,

except when  he tries to help.

He's all right, my dad.

My dad's a great dancer,

and a brilliant singer.

He's fantastic at soccer,

and he makes me laugh. A lot.

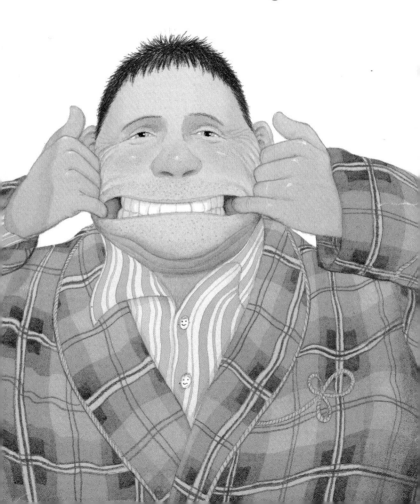

I love my dad.
And you know what?

HE LOVES ME!

(And he always will.)